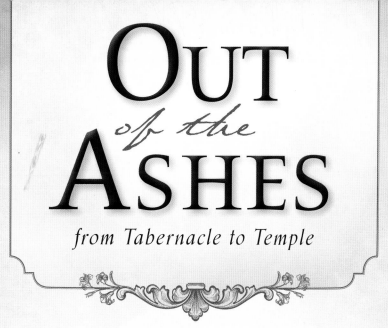

OUT *of the* ASHES

from Tabernacle to Temple

The glory of this latter house shall be greater than of the former, saith the Lord of hosts: and in this place will I give peace.

Haggai 2:9

To all those in the midst of the refiner's fire.
—J. D.

To Heavenly Father, who loves us all.
—W. O.

Though this story is a fictional account based on the experience of the Charles Eugene Fletcher family,
it is a tribute to the generations of families who have ties to the Provo Tabernacle, now the Provo City Center Temple.

Text © 2015 Judy Fletcher Davis

All artwork © Wilson J. Ong. For more information, please visit www.wilsonong.com.

Jacket and book design by Melyssa Ferguson © 2015 Covenant Communications, Inc.

Published by Covenant Communications, Inc.
American Fork, Utah

Printed in China
First Printing: September 2015

21 20 19 18 17 16 15   10 9 8 7 6 5 4 3 2 1

ISBN: 978-1-62108-718-2

OUT *of the* ASHES

from *Tabernacle* to *Temple*

BASED ON A TRUE STORY

Written by

Judy Fletcher Davis

Illustrated by

Wilson J. Ong

Covenant
Communications, Inc.

"I'm sad," a young boy said to his mother, crying softly.

"You're sad? Can we make it better?" his mother asked as she gently gathered him in her arms.

"No. Everything is ruined," he sobbed.

"Well, I don't know about that . . ." she said, hugging him closer. "I know someone who felt sad like this once, and things turned out for the best for them in the end. Would you like to hear the story?"

The boy nodded tearfully, and his mother began.

As one whom his mother comforteth, so will I comfort you; and ye shall be comforted.

Isaiah 66:13

Long ago, a young boy traveled across the plains to the Salt Lake Valley, where he planted crops, beat away crickets, and gave thanks with his family for the miracle of the seagulls.

As a young man, he moved to Provo, where he learned carpentry and built a church, a courthouse, and a home for his wife and children. He also worked on the new tabernacle—the grandest building in Utah Valley.

For we are labourers together with God: ye are God's husbandry, ye are God's building . . . As a wise masterbuilder, I have laid the foundation . . . which is Jesus Christ.

1 Corinthians 3:9–11

When it was finally finished, the tabernacle had five tall towers, forty arched windows, twenty-six pillars, four winding staircases, one giant pipe organ, and an abundance of finely crafted woodwork, which the carpenter had helped carve.

Let them make me a sanctuary; that I may dwell among them
. . . after the pattern of the tabernacle.

Exodus 25: 8–9

During the tabernacle's dedication, the carpenter did not hear the words of the ceremony because he had lost his hearing to disease. He had also lost two of his children through the years. He ached for what he'd once had, but as he admired the beautiful craftsmanship surrounding him, the Spirit of the Lord filled the tabernacle, and the carpenter felt peace.

I will hear what God the Lord will speak: for he will speak peace unto his people.

Psalms 85:8

Years later, the carpenter's son, a young bachelor, attended Church meetings in the tabernacle. As he listened to the sermon one day, he felt something hit him on the head—a red rose! He turned around to see a beautiful young lady acting innocent but blushing terribly. The Spirit of the Lord filled the tabernacle, and the bachelor and young lady felt peace. They fell in love and were soon married.

Throughout your generations at the door of the tabernacle . . .
I will meet you, to speak there unto thee.

Exodus 29:42

Years later, their son enlisted as a soldier and saw many horrible things in a war overseas. When he returned home, he attended patriotic events in the tabernacle. As he gathered with the community, the Spirit of the Lord filled the tabernacle, and he felt peace.

God is our refuge and strength, a very present help in trouble. Therefore will not we fear . . . . He maketh wars to cease unto the end of the earth; he breaketh the bow, and cutteth the spear in sunder; he burneth the chariot in the fire. Be still, and know that I am God.

Psalms 46: 1–2, 9–10

Years later, the soldier's daughter performed violin concertos in the tabernacle. As the beautiful music sang through the concert hall, the Spirit of the Lord filled the tabernacle, and the audience felt peace.

Come with singing . . . and everlasting joy shall
be upon their head: they shall obtain gladness and joy;
and sorrow and mourning shall flee away. I, even I,
am he that comforteth you.
Isaiah 51:11–12

Then, one night, the roof of the tabernacle caught fire! Firemen raced to the scene and fought desperately to control the blaze, but the burning roof collapsed, and flames destroyed the building.

When through fiery trials thy pathway shall lie, My grace, all sufficient, shall be thy supply. The flame shall not hurt thee; I only design . . . Thy dross to consume and thy gold to refine.
"How Firm a Foundation," Hymns, *no. 85*

The tabernacle was ruined. Only its rock foundation and outer walls remained, standing bravely around a dark cavity of ashes. The violinist, as well as the community, was devastated. They all mourned the loss of their historic gathering place.

For the mountains shall depart, and the hills be removed;
but my kindness shall not depart from thee, neither shall
the covenant of my peace be removed . . . . Behold, I have
created the smith that bloweth the coals in the fire, and that
bringeth forth an instrument for his work.

Isaiah 54:10, 16

Yet as crews searched through the ashes, they found a symbol of hope—a painting of Jesus Christ with His arms outstretched had miraculously survived the flames. The Spirit of the Lord filled the tabernacle, and everyone felt peace.

I will not leave you comfortless: I will come to you.
John 14:18

A few months later, the prophet announced that the tabernacle would be rebuilt—as a temple! Reconstruction began, transforming the ashes into a grand building with tall towers, arched windows, and finely crafted woodwork, just like before— but this time it also included a baptismal font in the basement, sealing rooms off the corridors, and a beautiful celestial room on the upper floor.

I will return, and will build again the tabernacle . . . which is fallen down; and I will build again the ruins thereof, and I will set it up: That the residue of men might seek after the Lord.
Acts 15:16–17

During the dedication ceremony, the violinist listened as the building was sanctified as an eternal gathering place. Though she could no longer perform concertos there, she could be an instrument in the Lord's work of uniting families forever. As she admired the beautiful craftsmanship surrounding her, the Spirit of the Lord filled the temple, and she felt peace.

That thy holy presence may be continually in this house; and that all people who shall enter upon the threshold of the Lord's house may feel thy power, and feel constrained to acknowledge that thou hast sanctified it, and that it is thy house, a place of thy holiness.

D&C 109:12–13

"That was you, wasn't it, Mom?" the boy asked as his mother finished her story.

"Yes, son, and the carpenter was your great-great-grandfather."

"And it turned out all right in the end?" the boy asked.

"Even better," his mother assured him.

As the boy thought about the new temple, the Spirit of the Lord filled his heart, and he felt peace.

For the Lord shall comfort Zion: he will comfort all her waste places; and he will make her wilderness like Eden, and her desert like the garden of the Lord.

Isaiah 51:3

He knew that one day he would escort a beautiful young lady through corridors of finely crafted woodwork to a special room, where generations of family would gather to watch them be married for all eternity . . .

And they were married, and given in marriage, and were blessed according to the multitude of the promises which the Lord had made unto them.

4 Nephi 1:11

. . . in the historic building that had risen out of the ashes to become a holy temple.

To give unto them beauty for ashes,
the oil of joy for mourning, the garment of
praise for the spirit of heaviness . . .
that he might be glorified.

Isaiah 61:3